·FOREVER·FRIENDS·™

"Twice around the Moon"

by Deborah Jones.

© The Andrew Brownsword Collection.
All rights reserved.
First published in 1996 by World International Ltd.,
Deanway Technology Centre, Wilmslow Road, Handforth,
Cheshire, SK9 3FB. Printed in Great Britain.
ISBN 0 7498 2884 6

The Forever Friends are all playing in the attic.

Little Bear and her hobby horse are having a race with the Duck on wheels.

Big Bear is helping Rabbit with her colouring-in.

Tiny Bear has nothing to do. "I'm bored!" says Tiny Bear.

"Go and find something to do," says Big Bear. "There are lots of toys in the attic."

Tiny Bear wanders off, mumbling to himself, "I'm bored, I'm <u>very</u> bored!"

All of a sudden he sees something extremely large, covered with a dustsheet in the corner of the attic. "I wonder what this could be?" he thinks as he lifts the edge of the dustsheet. He tugs with all his might to reveal...

...a beautiful Rocking Horse!

"Come and see what I've found!" shouts Tiny Bear.

Big Bear and Rabbit run over to the corner of the attic.

"What a beautiful Rocking Horse!" says Rabbit.

"Thank you," says the Rocking Horse.

Big Bear helps Rabbit and Tiny Bear on to the back of the Horse and then climbs into the saddle himself.

The Horse rocks as they all shout, "Giddy-up! Giddy-up!"

"Now we can have a pretend race with Little Bear and the Duck," says Tiny Bear.

The Forever Friends rock the Horse faster and faster. Little Bear rushes round on her hobby horse. "Giddy-up!" she yells. "I'm winning, I'm winning!"

The Forever Friends jump up and down in the saddle and Rocking Horse lurches up and down alarmingly on his rockers.

"Faster, faster!" says Rabbit at the top of her voice.

Suddenly the Horse lifts his hooves and gallops free of his rockers!

The Forever Friends hold on to each other tightly as the Horse leaps and bounds around the attic.

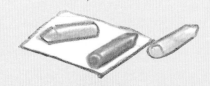

The Rocking Horse is racing around and building up a lot of speed. All of a sudden he trips up on a playing brick and hurtles through the wooden frame into the blackness of the chalkboard!

"Oh dear," says Big Bear. "What shall we do now?"

"Head for that yellow thing," says Little Bear. "I think it might be the moon. I've always wanted to go to the moon!"

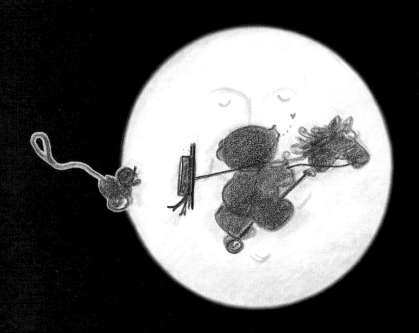

Little Bear and Duck follow the Rocking Horse
into the chalkboard. As she passes the face of the
moon Little Bear blows him a kiss. It lands high
on his cheek.

"Twice around the moon," shouts Rabbit,
"and the first one back to the attic is the winner
of the race!"

It's neck and neck as the horses reach the attic. But just at the last moment the Duck flies into the lead...

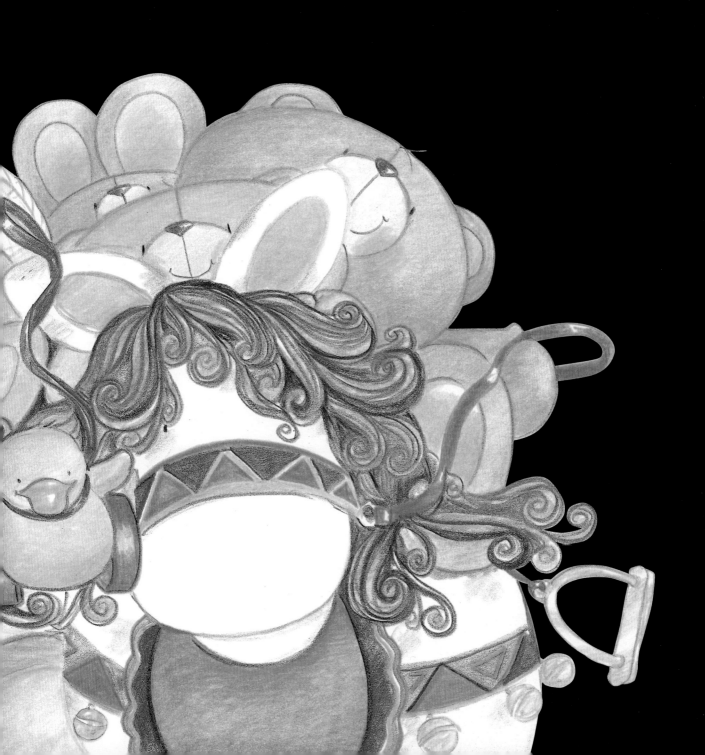

...and arrives back in the attic first. "I'm the winner!" he says proudly.

Big Bear helps the Horse back on to his rockers and covers him with his dustsheet.

"Thank you," says the Horse.

"Thank **you**," say the Friends. "We had a wonderful time!"

"Come on," says Big Bear. "It's getting late. Time to get into the basket!"

The little ones scurry off to their basket. As Big Bear turns to follow he notices that the chalk moon has disappeared from the chalkboard. "That's strange!" he thinks.

"Big Bear, come quickly!" say the little ones. "Look! Look!" they say, pointing to the window above the basket. "It's our chalk moon up there in the sky!"

Big Bear stares into the blackness and smiles. "Say goodnight to our moon," he says.

"Goodnight, moon!"
The chalk moon winks...
"Goodnight, chalk moon. Goodnight!"